PUFFIN BOOKS

Mr Majei...

Humphrey Carpenter i........ of the Mr Majeika stories for children. He was born and educated in Oxford and worked for the BBC before becoming a full-time writer in 1975. He has published award-winning biographies of J. R. R. Tolkien, C. S. Lewis, W. H. Auden, Benjamin Britten and others, and is the co-author, with his wife, Mari Prichard, of *The Oxford Companion to Children's Literature*. From 1994 to 1996 he directed the Cheltenham Festival of Literature. He has written plays for radio and the theatre, including a dramatization of *Gulliver's Travels* (1995), and for many years ran a young people's drama group, the Mushy Pea Theatre Company. He has two daughters.

Some other books by Humphrey Carpenter

MR MAJEIKA
MR MAJEIKA AND THE DINNER LADY
MR MAJEIKA AND THE GHOST TRAIN
MR MAJEIKA AND THE
HAUNTED HOTEL
MR MAJEIKA AND THE MUSIC TEACHER
MR MAJEIKA AND THE
SCHOOL BOOK WEEK
MR MAJEIKA AND THE
SCHOOL INSPECTOR
MR MAJEIKA AND THE SCHOOL PLAY
MR MAJEIKA'S POSTBAG
MR MAJEIKA AND THE
SCHOOL CARETAKER

THE PUFFIN BOOK OF CLASSIC
CHILDREN'S STORIES (Ed.)

Humphrey Carpenter

Mr Majeika
Vanishes

Illustrated by Frank Rodgers

PUFFIN BOOKS

With thanks to children from the Willows School and Stratford Preparatory School, Stratford-upon-Avon, for helping to invent these goings-on at Wizardford-upon-Sky.

PUFFIN BOOKS

Published by the Penguin Group
Penguin Books Ltd, 27 Wrights Lane, London W8 5TZ, England
Penguin Putnam Inc., 375 Hudson Street, New York,
New York 10014, USA
Penguin Books Australia Ltd, Ringwood, Victoria, Australia
Penguin Books Canada Ltd, 10 Alcorn Avenue, Toronto,
Ontario, Canada M4V 3B2
Penguin Books (NZ) Ltd, Cnr Rosedale and Airborne Roads, Albany,
Auckland, New Zealand

Penguin Books Ltd, Registered Offices: Harmondsworth,
Middlesex, England

First published by Viking 1997
Published in Puffin Books 1998
1 3 5 7 9 10 8 6 4 2

Set in Palatino

Made and printed in England by Clays Ltd, St Ives plc

British Library Cataloguing in Publication Data
A CIP catalogue record for this book is available from the British Library
ISBN 0–140–37840–5

1. Hamish Comes Out Top

It was the beginning of a new term at St Barty's School, and the end of the holidays, but no one in Class Three minded, because they had the most exciting teacher in the world.

Mr Majeika had been a wizard before he became a schoolmaster, and though he wasn't supposed to do magic nowadays, you never knew what would happen in Class Three. People kept getting turned into things like frogs and lobsters, or sometimes the whole class went off on a strange trip, time-travelling, or meeting ghosts. Some days were quite ordinary, but you could count on at least one exciting thing happening each term.

The only person who didn't love being taught by Mr Majeika was Hamish Bigmore, the silliest boy in the class. So Thomas and Pete, and their friend Jody, began to think that something was wrong when they arrived for assembly, at the start of the first morning of term, and saw that Hamish had a nasty smile on his face.

"What's up, Hamish?" asked Thomas. "Have you had a nice holiday?"

"Pretty boring," snapped Hamish. "But I'm going to have a really great term. Just you wait and see!" And he laughed a nasty laugh.

Mr Potter came into the school hall, and went on to the platform with the other teachers. "Where's Mr Majeika?"

whispered Jody. "It's not like him to be late."

"And who's that woman standing next to Mr Potter?" whispered Thomas. "I'm sure I've seen her somewhere before."

"Of course you have," said Pete. "It's –" But at that moment, Mr Potter called for silence.

"I hope everybody had a lovely

holiday," he said. "We have a change to the staff this term. Mr Majeika has left us, and he is being replaced by –"

There was a loud groan from everyone in Class Three – everyone except Hamish Bigmore, who was smirking all over his face. "Told you so," he said to Thomas, Pete and Jody. "It's the best news for years and years and years."

"No it isn't," said Jody. She felt like crying, and indeed Melanie, who cried all the time, had already burst into tears, and was howling at the top of her voice.

"Boo-hoo!" she sobbed. "What's happened to Mr Majeika? He wouldn't have left us without saying goodbye. There must be something wrong."

"Be quiet, all of you," called out Mr Potter. "There's nothing wrong at all. Mr Majeika has retired. He was quite old, you know."

Thomas, Pete and Jody looked at each other. "He wasn't old at all," said Pete. "There's something funny going on. And I bet Hamish is behind it."

"Quiet!" called Mr Potter again. "I haven't finished. As I was saying, Mr Majeika has already been replaced. And I have some very good news for you. It's not easy to find good teachers at short notice, but among our parents we have one person who used to be a teacher, and now I'm very pleased to say she's decided to start teaching again. Many of you will have recognized her, here on the platform. Class Three are very lucky, because she's going to be their new teacher. I am talking, of course, about Hamish's mother, Mrs Dulcie Bigmore."

There was one loud shout of "Hooray!", which came, of course, from Hamish. Everyone else groaned, and Pete even muttered "Boo!"

"That's rude," Thomas said to him. "We don't know what Hamish's mum will be like as a teacher. Maybe she'll be very good."

"Maybe the sky will turn green," said Pete. "If you ask me, there's only one person who's going to enjoy being taught by Mrs Bigmore. And I bet you can guess who that is."

It didn't take long for Pete to be proved right. As soon as Class Three had settled down for the first lesson, Mrs Bigmore said, "Good morning, everyone, and this morning we're going to start with Maths."

"No we're not!" shouted Hamish.

"Maths is boring. I'm not going to do any Maths this term."

"Oh, but Hamish, *please*," said his mother. "Mr Potter has given me a list of things I must teach you all, and Maths is at the top of it."

"Give me the list," said Hamish, snatching it from his mother. He looked through it. "Maths, English, story-writing, reading aloud, French, Geography, History – this is rubbish!" And he tore the list up into little bits.

"Now, Hamish, you're really being very naughty," said Mrs Bigmore.

"So what are you going to do about it?" asked Hamish, pushing his face very close to his mother's. "Eh? Eh?"

Mrs Bigmore backed away from him nervously. "I – I – I won't give you any chocolate at break time," she said feebly.

"You won't need to," shouted Hamish,

"because I've already pinched it from your handbag." And out of his desk he took an enormous bar of chocolate, and began munching it at once.

"Oh dear," sighed Mrs Bigmore. "I should never have taken on this job."

"Please can I make a suggestion?" asked Jody. "Mr Majeika always used to begin each term by telling us to write down what we've done in the holidays. Shall we do that?"

"What a good idea," said Mrs Bigmore. "But I expect Hamish won't want to."

"Oh yes I will," said Hamish, grinning. "Here goes." And for the next ten minutes, to everyone's surprise, he was quiet and well-behaved, writing on a piece of paper.

"Time's up," said Mrs Bigmore after the ten minutes were over. "Who'd like to read out what they've written?"

Hamish's hand shot up, but Mrs
Bigmore said, "We'll keep you till last,
Hamish, sweetie. It's always a good idea
to keep the best till last."

18

Thomas and Pete looked at each other. "What a wonderful term this is going to be," said Thomas.

Melanie read out hers first. It was all about the baby rabbits she had at home, and what she gave them to eat, and how much she liked playing with them. When she had finished, Hamish said some very rude things to her about it, and of course she cried.

One by one, everyone in Class Three took a turn at reading what they had written. Some people had been away for interesting holidays. Someone else had been in hospital for an operation. Pandora Green had moved house, and she had written a funny piece about how her small brother had got lost during the move, and had finally been found asleep in a laundry basket in the movers' van.

Finally, it was Hamish's turn. "Like my

mum said, the best comes last," he remarked, grinning. Then he read out: "'This holiday I had a very exciting time, because I was captured by aliens from outer space. They were little green men who came out of a flying saucer, and they kidnapped me and took me off to Mars, but I stole their ray guns and shot them all dead, splat, splat, splat, splat. Then I

steered their flying saucer back to Earth. The end, by Hamish Bigmore.'"

"Hamish, darling, that was wonderful," cooed his mother. "Such imagination! Such wonderful writing! I'm sure my darling Hamish is going to be a brilliant and famous author when he grows up."

"I wish aliens from Mars *would* capture him," muttered Pete. "And we were supposed to write what really happened. I hope she makes him do it again."

But of course Mrs Bigmore didn't. "Hamish gets top marks," she said, just as the bell rang for break time. "Well done, Hamish, darling!"

As they all went into the playground, Jody said to Thomas and Pete: "This is awful. We've simply got to find out what's happened to Mr Majeika. I'm sure Melanie's right – he wouldn't have left us on purpose without saying goodbye."

2. The Silly Crime Squad

"The first thing to do," said Pete, "is to discover where he lives." They went and asked the school secretary, and she gave them an address about half a mile away.

"That sounds very ordinary," said Thomas, as he and Pete and Jody set off to look for it, when school had finished that afternoon. "I thought Mr Majeika would have a really weird, wizardly sort of home. Maybe a hollow tree, or a haunted castle."

"Well, we've only got the address, 27 Lower Barty Street," said Jody. "Who knows, when we get there, it may be a tree or a castle."

"Or maybe a tent," said Pete. "I think a wizard like Mr Majeika ought to live in a multi-coloured tent, spangled like the stars, which glows mysteriously in the night, and makes a faint humming sound."

But 27 Lower Barty Street turned out not to be a hollow tree, or a haunted castle, or a humming tent, just a very ordinary house, though it was rather tall and narrow.

There was a name under the doorbell. It said "Mrs Carrot". "What a funny name for Mr Majeika to give himself," said Thomas. "Perhaps he's trying to hide from someone."

"Don't be silly," said Pete. "I expect Mrs

Carrot is the lady who owns the house. Mr Majeika probably just has one floor of it."

He was right about Mrs Carrot. When she came to the door, she had carrot-red hair, and she said that yes, Mr Majeika was one of her lodgers. "But he's not here now, my friend. He went off one night last week."

"Went off?" said Jody. "What do you

mean? Walked out of the house and didn't come back?"

"Oh, it was much odder than that, dear," said Mrs Carrot. "Some people came and took him away."

"People? What sort of people?" asked Thomas. "It wasn't a boy called Hamish Bigmore, was it?"

"And maybe a nasty old witch called Wilhelmina Worlock?" added Thomas. "She's always trying to do some harm to Mr Majeika."

"No, dear, I don't think there was a witch among them," said Mrs Carrot. "But why don't you all come up and have a look at his room? Maybe he's left a note for you."

They went up the stairs behind Mrs Carrot. "Has he only got one room?" asked Thomas.

"Yes, dear. He lived very quietly, and

never made any noise. Only, sometimes I would hear him chanting to himself, in a sort of sing-song voice. I expect he was speaking poetry."

"Spells, I reckon," whispered Jody to Pete.

They reached the top of the stairs, and opened a door. Mr Majeika's room was in the rooftop, and had a nice view over the town. There was a wizard's hat on top of the bookcase, and some big books which looked like spell-books, and something that might be a magic wand, but mostly it looked very ordinary. It was also very untidy. Clothes and papers and other things had been thrown all over the floor.

"Mr Majeika is always very tidy at school," said Jody. "I'm surprised he lets his room get into such a mess."

"Oh, but he doesn't, my friend," said Mrs Carrot. "I often come in here to do a

bit of sweeping and dusting, and I've never seen it in such a mess as this. I thought I could hear a bit of a struggle going on when they took him away."

"Who was it, Mrs Carrot?" asked Thomas. "What did they look like? And did they come in a car?"

"No, dear," said Mrs Carrot. "They came on a magic carpet."

"Goodness!" said Jody. "Weren't you surprised?"

"Well, I suppose I was a bit," said Mrs Carrot, "but I'm used to lodgers having peculiar friends. Mr Christmas, who used to live across the landing, had a pet bear which he kept in the bathroom – quite a nuisance it was, when you wanted to take a bath – and Miss Hoopoe on the floor below used to be an astronaut in America, and once one of her friends came to visit her in a sort of spaceship. So I wasn't as surprised by the magic carpet as some people might have been."

"Was it a very big one?" asked Pete.

"Big enough for five or six of them to sit on it," said Mrs Carrot. "There was a sort of ghost in a white sheet, and a vampire, and an Egyptian mummy, and a space alien, and even a dinosaur. And they were all in uniform, like policemen. Come to think of it, there was a revolving light on the carpet – it was like a Hallowe'en pumpkin with a candle inside – which was going round and round like the blue light on a police car."

"Look!" said Jody. She had been picking up the clothes and other things that were lying about the room, and had found a piece of paper. "It's Mr Majeika's handwriting."

On it he had written, in a great hurry, by the look of it: "Someone has played a trick on me and the Wizards' Silly Crime Squad is taking me away. Please help. Try the bike."

"I've heard of the Serious Crime Squad," said Thomas, "so I suppose the Silly Crime Squad is for catching people who've done silly things. But it's not like Mr Majeika to commit a crime."

"He says someone played a trick,"

pointed out Pete. "But what does he mean by 'Try the bike'? Does he have a bicycle, Mrs Carrot?"

"No, dear," said Mrs Carrot. "He always used to walk to school."

"But the first time he came to school," said Jody excitedly, "it was on a magic carpet which turned into –"

"A bike!" shouted Thomas and Pete.

They recognized Mr Majeika's bicycle at once in the school bike shed. It had strange red and green markings. "I'm surprised no one has stolen it," said Thomas. "It's not locked up."

"The thing to do," said Jody, "is to try and get it to change itself back into a magic carpet. Then we could ask it to take us to Mr Majeika, and we can rescue him."

"You try, Jody," said Thomas. "You're good at remembering Mr Majeika's spells."

"Yes, there was that time when you managed to make a Hoover, and a wheelchair, and even a van fly," said Pete. "I bet you can make this become a magic carpet again."

But she couldn't. However many words and phrases Jody repeated, that she had heard Mr Majeika say when he was doing magic, and however often she waved her hands over the bike, or clicked her fingers, nothing happened. The bike just went on being a bike.

"This is awful," said Thomas. "I'm sure Mr Majeika thought we could do it. Otherwise he wouldn't have left the note for us. And we *know* he needs rescuing."

"Wait a minute," said Pete. "The note didn't say, 'Try turning the bike back into a magic carpet.' It just said, 'Try the bike.' So why don't we?"

"All right," said Jody. "You try it." So Pete got on it, and rode around the playground. It was quite a nice bike to ride, except that the back tyre was almost flat.

"You've got to pedal it just as hard as an

ordinary bike. I'd have thought a wizard's bike would pedal itself. You know, you could just tell it: 'Take me very fast down

the road,' and it would. Oh – help!" He
shouted these last words because
suddenly the bike did exactly that – took
him very fast out of the playground and
down the road, without his even having
to steer it.

"Tell it to bring you back again," called
Thomas. So Pete gave the bike its orders,

and sure enough, it whizzed back all by itself.

"I think we're getting somewhere," said Pete. "Now, if I were to say to it, 'Take me to Mr Majeika –'" Again, he broke off, gasping, because the bike had risen very fast in the air. It was going up and up and up!

"Go down again!" Pete shouted at it. "I want to take the others with me." The bike obeyed, dropping down into the playground. "Now," he said to Jody, "you have the seat, and I'll sit on the crossbar, and Thomas can sit on the carrier over the back wheel."

"Why do I get the worst place to sit?" Thomas grumbled at his brother.

"You don't," said Pete. "I get the worst. Ouch! This crossbar is very hard indeed to sit on. But off we go. Now, bike, you can really do it. Take us to Mr Majeika!"

3. A Very Unusual Fence

Pete was feeling very airsick indeed,
Thomas was white in the face and
holding on very tightly, and even Jody,
who had the bike seat and Pete to grip on
to, looked very shaky as the flying bicycle
whizzed through the clouds and then
suddenly came to rest on a patch of grass.

"Well, I'm never doing that again," said
Thomas, gasping for breath as he climbed
off the bike on to a patch of grass.

"You're going to have to," said Pete.

"Otherwise how will you get back to Earth?"

Thomas looked around him. "Aren't we still on Earth?" he said. "There's ordinary ground, and grass, and things like that, and trees."

"But just go to the edge and look down," said Jody, pointing to where the grass suddenly stopped.

Thomas went across, and found himself peering down through the clouds. "Gosh!" he said. "We're on a land in the sky. Like in *Jack and the Beanstalk*. I wonder if there are dangerous giants up here," he added nervously.

"I don't think so," said Pete, pointing. A large notice said: "Welcome to Wizardford-upon-Sky. No parking of magic carpets. No bicycles allowed within the city gates."

"Wizardford-upon-Sky," repeated

Thomas. "That sounds like the town where all the wizards live. Gosh, that's probably where we'll find Mr Majeika. Hooray! Then we can bring him home with us."

But Jody was frowning. "I don't think it's as simple as that," she said. "Look!"

Wizardford-upon-Sky was surrounded by a high fence, with spikes on top. In the

middle of the fence was a big gatehouse, with a pair of huge gates. They were both shut tight, and a big sign said "Closed".

"That's very odd," said Thomas. "I've never seen a town that was closed. When is it going to open again?"

"It's not!" snapped a voice. "It's closed for ever and ever and ever. Go away!"

"Who said that?" asked Thomas. "I didn't see anyone."

"I think a little window opened in the gate," said Jody, "and then shut again. And I thought I recognized the voice."

"So did I," said Pete. "It sounded like Hamish Bigmore. But how on earth could he have got up here?"

"If Wilhelmina Worlock is behind all this," said Jody, "and I suspect she is, then she could have brought Hamish with her. But let's go and see if it is him."

They went over to the gate, and banged

on it. They could see the little window that had opened for Hamish – if it was him – to shout through. But however hard they knocked, nobody answered.

"Oh dear," said Thomas. "This is useless. We'd better give up and go home."

"Certainly not," said Jody. "Look, the fence goes right round Wizardford. If we walk along it, we might find a hole in it."

They set off. Through the fence, they could see the town of Wizardford. There were a lot of very strangely shaped buildings, towers and domes and castles that looked haunted. But there seemed to be no one there at all. Everything was very quiet.

"It's very strange," said Pete. "I think this must be the headquarters of all the wizards, but there doesn't seem to be anyone moving about."

"Perhaps they're all asleep," said
Thomas. "Maybe they have a nap in the
daytime, and then come out at night."

"Maybe," said Jody. "But I think there's
something peculiar about it. And, oh dear,
there don't seem to be any gaps in the
fence."

They had walked a long way, but the

fence just went on and on, and as Jody
said, there were no gaps at all. After a
while they got tired. Pete and Jody sat
down on the ground, and Thomas leaned
against the fence.

"There must be something we can do,"
sighed Jody. "Perhaps if we shouted Mr
Majeika's name, he might answer us.
Oh – Thomas – look what's happened to
your arms."

Thomas's back had been against the fence, and his elbows had been poking a little way through it. He looked at them. They had gone all soft and rubbery. "Help!" he said. "Fetch a doctor!"

"Don't panic yet," said Jody. "Remember, this is the land of the wizards. A lot of peculiar things probably happen here. Let me try."

Very cautiously, she touched the fence. It didn't feel strange, but when she took her hand away, she found that it had gone all soft and flexible. "It's a bit frightening," she said, "but it gives me an idea. I think I'm going to see if I can't squeeze through the fence. If it makes us go all squidgy, it should be possible."

"But will we be squidgy for the rest of our lives?" asked Pete nervously.

"Who knows?" said Jody. "But we've got to rescue Mr Majeika, and even if it makes me squidgy for ever and ever, I'll do it!"

She put her head against the fence, and sure enough she felt it going soft. By pushing quite hard, she found that in a moment or two she had become completely soft, as if she were made of Plasticine. Still pushing, she found herself on the other side of the fence – and to her great relief, she immediately became normal again, and was able to stand up and walk about without collapsing in a soft heap. "Now it's your turn," she called to Thomas and Pete.

At first, they were both very nervous. Pete put his foot against the fence first, and then got frightened and took it away again. But it had already gone soft, so when he tried to stand on it, he fell over. "I think that's because you haven't come through the fence," said Jody. "I think if

you stay on that side, it'll go on being soft
for ever and ever."

So Pete shut his eyes, and pushed the
whole of his body against the fence, and
in a minute he found himself on the other
side, and back to normal.

Thomas came through more slowly, and
started playing games. "Look!" he
shouted out. "I can make my nose really

long. And my fingers all round and fat."
He was actually enjoying being a
Plasticine version of himself, twisting and
bending so that he started to look like
someone completely different.

When he finally came through the
fence, Pete started laughing. "What's the
matter?" asked Thomas.

"You're still that funny shape," said
Pete. "You've twisted and bent yourself
so much that it hasn't come straight
again."

"Gosh," said Thomas gloomily. "I don't
want to look like this for the rest of my
life."

"Don't worry," said Jody. "If you get
back into the fence again, I think you'll
find yourself softening up, and then you
can straighten yourself out."

Thomas tried it, and to his relief, it
worked. "Hey, this is really great," he

said. "We could have some real fun with it."

"You bet we could," said Pete, and for the next few minutes he and Thomas had a wonderful time bending themselves into the weirdest shapes. Pete managed to make himself into someone about six metres high, with a neck like a snake, and Thomas twisted his face so that he looked very strange. It was ages before Jody could persuade them to stop, and get back to their normal shapes.

"Honestly, you two," she complained. "You seem to have forgotten why we've come here. Don't you remember? I'm sure Mr Majeika is in real trouble. Somehow, we've got to find him."

4. Changing Jody

Inside the fence, Wizardford-upon-Sky looked even odder. Steam and strange-coloured smoke were coming out of the ground, and there were distant clunking and bubbling sounds. But no voices were to be heard, and Jody, Thomas and Pete had no idea where to begin looking.

"There's a notice over there," said Thomas. "Let's go and see what it says."

The notice was on the side of a peculiar-looking building shaped like a heart. It said "Love Potion Factory".

"What on earth does that mean?" asked Thomas.

"What do you think?" said Pete. "It's a factory where they make love potions. Surely you've heard of them?"

"Yes," said Thomas. "But I didn't think there really were such things as love potions."

"Of course there aren't," said Jody. "They're only in stories. The factory is obviously a fake."

"I wonder," said Pete. "Remember, we're in the land of the wizards, where anything can happen. Let's go in and find out."

They went through the doorway, which was heart-shaped like the building. Inside it was very dark, but there was romantic music playing, and it smelt like a perfume shop.

"Good afternoon, sirs, and good

afternoon, madam," said a silky, slinky voice. They peered into the darkness. Coming towards them, lit up by a strange pinkish light, was a very odd-looking woman. She had bright yellow hair, which tumbled down over her shoulders, very red lips (with the lipstick put on rather clumsily), a dress like an old bedspread, and dark glasses with glitter all over them, so that they couldn't see her face properly.

"Good afternoon, good afternoon," she repeated in a low purring voice. "Welcome to Madame Melisande's Potion Powerhouse. Does the girl you love hate the sight of you? Madame Melisande's Potion will make her fancy you like fury! Can't your boyfriend be bothered to kiss you goodnight? Madame Melisande's Potion will make him fall for you ferociously! Put a few drops in your friends' packed lunches and you'll find you're the most popular person in the school! Madame Melisande mends broken hearts, repairs romances and brings love into every life. Ha ha!"

Until these last two words, Madame Melisande had sounded just like the sort of lady who sells perfume and make-up in a big department store or chemist's shop. But when she said "Ha ha!" there was something different about her.

Jody, Thomas and Pete looked at each other, and they all said: "Hamish Bigmore!"

"Yah boo sucks!" shouted Hamish, and, still dressed at Madame Melisande, he ran away through the darkness. They heard a door banging shut behind him.

"It's very odd," said Jody, "that Hamish should be the only person around in Wizardford. I wonder what's happened to all the wizards?"

"Come on," said Pete, "let's go. Mr Majeika isn't in here."

But Thomas wasn't in so much of a hurry. "Do you think Hamish's love potion really works?" he asked.

Jody shook her head. "Not if Hamish made it," she said. "Anything that *he's* mixed up is more likely to make you feel sick than fall in love with somebody."

"I wonder," said Pete. "He can't have been up here in Wizardford very long –

he was at school only a short time ago. So I don't think he'd have had time to mess around with stuff in here. Probably it's a real love potion factory, and he's just dressing up in order to make fools of us."

"In that case," said Thomas, picking up a bottle, "I want to know if it works." The bottle was labelled *Melisande's Strongest: one drop and you lose your heart*.

"Of course it doesn't," said Jody. "Love potions are just things in stories. There couldn't really be such a thing."

"Why not?" asked Pete. "Until we met Mr Majeika, we didn't believe in magic. Now we know it's true. So perhaps this is true too."

"I vote we try it," said Thomas.

"*You* can," said Pete. "I'm not touching it."

"Me neither," said Jody.

"Well, I don't see why it should be me," said Thomas. "Let's toss a coin for it."

"But there are three of us," said Pete, "and the coin only has two sides."

"Well," said Thomas, "we can start by tossing between Pete and me. Then it can be the winner against Jody."

"You mean the loser," said Pete. "But all right, that's fair enough."

So Thomas took a coin out of his pocket and tossed, and Pete called "Heads", and it was tails, so Thomas tossed against

Jody, and Jody called "Tails", and it was tails, so Jody was going to have to try the love potion.

"I don't want to," she said.

"Too bad," said Thomas. "That's how the tossing came out. Here – there's some sugar-lumps in this box. I'll pour a drop of *Melisande's Strongest* on to it, and you can eat the sugar, and we'll see what happens."

Jody made a face, but when Thomas had put the love potion on to the sugar-lump, she ate it up.

"Quick!" shouted Pete to Thomas. "We've got to hide! Otherwise she'll fall in love with whichever of us she notices first, when she's digested the potion. That's how it usually works in stories."

So they hid behind a table, and waited for Jody to feel the effects of the potion.

"I feel just the same as usual," said Jody,

after a few moments. "I don't think it
works."

"We can't tell," said Pete. "You haven't
seen anybody yet, so goodness knows
what will happen when you do."

At that moment they heard a door
opening. Out of the darkness, in his

normal school clothes, came Hamish Bigmore.

"Hello, Jody," he said, grinning a nasty grin.

Jody gasped. "Hamish!" she cooed. "I've never realized before how beautiful you are!"

It took Thomas and Pete ten minutes of struggling with Jody to get her out of the Love Potion Factory. "Hamish!" she kept shouting. "I can't live without you! Let's get married at once, and we'll live in a pretty cottage with roses round the door, and raise a family of little Hamishes. Oh, how lucky your sons and daughters will be, to look just like you."

For a bit, Hamish had stood there laughing, and then he ran away. He didn't really seem to enjoy Jody being in love with him – any more than *she* would

have enjoyed it if she'd not been under the influence of the love potion.

"Let's hope it wears off in a few hours," Thomas said to Pete.

"I wouldn't count on it," said Pete. "It was called Strongest, wasn't it? She may be like this for years and years."

"If only we could find Mr Majeika," said Thomas. "He'd know what to do."

"Look!" said Pete. He pointed at a

building with a notice outside that said "Behaviour Changing Factory".

"What does that mean?" asked Thomas.

"Just what it says, I suppose," answered Pete. "It must be a factory for changing how people behave. Come on, let's go and have a look."

"But I can't leave my wonderful, handsome Hamish," sobbed Jody, as they led her away from the Love Potion Factory. "Oh, Hamish, you're such a dreamboat, such a hunk!"

When they got to the Behaviour Changing Factory, Thomas peered through the door before they went in. "Hamish might be here now," he said. "And I've had quite enough of him!"

But there was no one inside. Unlike the Love Potion Factory, it was brightly lit. There were lots of tables, on which were set little bottles of crystals. These were all

labelled "Behaviour Changing No. 1",
"Behaviour Changing No. 2", and so on.

"It doesn't say what sort of behaviour it
changes you into," complained Pete.

"Oh, Hamish, Hamish," sighed Jody,
"send me your signed photograph, and I
will pin it above my bed, and blow kisses
to it every night before I go to sleep."

"We've got to do something to bring her
to her senses," said Thomas. "Let's just
give her a taste from one of these bottles,
and see what happens."

"Look," said Pete, "there's some on that
table by the door which do say what's in
them." He went over and read the labels.
They said: "Sensible Mixture. To stop silly
behaviour of all kinds. Take one
teaspoonful twice daily."

"That's just what we want," said
Thomas. He undid one of the bottles,
found a spoon, and poured some Sensible

Mixture into it. "Swallow that, Jody," he said, "and you'll feel much better."

"The only thing that would make me feel better," said Jody passionately, "would be pressing my lips on Hamish's cheek." But she swallowed the Sensible Mixture.

The moment she'd done so, she blinked. "What's happening?" she asked in a strange voice.

"You're stopping being in love with Hamish," said Pete hopefully.

"Yes, I'm stopping being in love with Hamish," echoed Jody. "I can't be in love with him," she went on, her voice changing, "because I *am* Hamish. Ha ha!" She went on, sounding just like Hamish now, "I'm the naughtiest boy in Class Three, I hate Mr Majeika, and my best friend is Wilhelmina Worlock."

"Oh, stop it, Jody," said Thomas. "Stop fooling around."

"I don't think she is fooling," said Pete,

looking worried. "Can't you see? Her face is changing, and she's starting to look exactly like Hamish."

"You bet she is," said a familiar voice. It was the real Hamish, peeping round the door of the Behaviour Changing Factory. "I got my friend Wilhelmina to make up that Sensible Mixture, specially so that one of you would drink it and turn into me! And there's not much you can do about it. Those Love Potions wear off after just a few hours, but the Behaviour Mixtures last for ever."

"We've *got* to find Mr Majeika," said Thomas frantically. He started shouting. "Mr Majeika! Mr Majeika! Can you hear us?"

And to Thomas and Pete's surprise, a very tiny voice answered, from what sounded like a long way away: "Yes, I can."

5. Bottled Up

They went on calling his name, and Mr Majeika kept replying in a tiny voice, but Thomas and Pete couldn't tell where it was coming from. "You'll never find him," sneered Hamish. "Silly old Mr Majeika, he's hidden away where no one will discover him. Good riddance to him!"

"Yes, good riddance to stupid Mr Majeika," said Jody, in a voice just like Hamish's. "Who wants a silly old wizard to teach Class Three? Let's have Wilhelmina Worlock!"

"I'm sure Wilhelmina is behind this," said Thomas. "But Mr Majeika can't be far. I can hear him so clearly."

"Let's try this cupboard," said Pete. "I've got an idea his voice might be coming from there."

He opened a cupboard near the door of the Behaviour Changing Factory. Inside there were several shelves, and on each of these was a row of small bottles.

"No, there's no room for him in there," said Thomas.

But Pete was peering closely at the bottles. "Come and look," he called. "I can see tiny faces inside them."

Thomas looked closely. "Gosh!" he said. "You're right. Tiny, tiny faces, and they all look rather like wizards."

"They are," said Mr Majeika's voice,

which was very close to them now. "All of us are here, every single wizard who lives in Wizardford-upon-Sky. And if you look at the third bottle from the left on the second shelf from the top, you'll see me."

Sure enough, there was Mr Majeika, very tiny, and squashed into a bottle with a cork jammed tight into the top.

"Poor Mr Majeika," said Thomas. "If we take the cork out, can you squeeze through the neck, and will you be able to get back to your own size again?"

"I'm afraid not," said Mr Majeika. "A very powerful spell put me in here, and it'll take a spell just as powerful to get me out again. I bet you can guess who did it."

"Wilhelmina Worlock?" said Pete and Thomas together.

The tiny Mr Majeika nodded. "You'd better hear the whole story," he said.

"Wait a minute," said Pete. "What's

happened to Hamish?" They looked
around, but Hamish had disappeared.
Jody was wandering up and down
outside the Behaviour Changing Factory,
saying Hamish-like things in Hamish's
voice – "Zoom, zoom, I want a splat-gun
that will splat everyone I see. And I hope
boring old Mr Majeika stays in his bottle
for ever."

"Tell us what happened, Mr Majeika," said Thomas.

"Well," said Mr Majeika, "the trouble started with my Wizard's Licence. Did you know that all wizards have to have licences to do magic? It's like a driving licence, for driving a car. I still had mine, even though I wasn't supposed to do magic down at St Barty's, and I thought it would be years and years before it ran out. The date on it said: 'This licence expires in the year 5000'."

"That's more than three thousand years from now," said Pete.

"Exactly," continued Mr Majeika. "So I couldn't understand what was going on when, one evening, the Wizards' Silly Crime Squad raided my bed-sitting room, where I was living, and asked me to show them my licence."

"We heard all about the Silly Crime

Squad from your landlady, Mrs Carrot,"
said Thomas.

"I think she was rather upset," said Mr
Majeika, "when all those ghosts and
vampires and aliens tramped up her stairs
to the top floor. But she wasn't nearly as
upset as me, when I gave them my
Wizard's Licence, and they pointed out
that it had expired last month."

"I thought you said it had three
thousand years to run," said Thomas.

"It did," said Mr Majeika, "until someone altered it. The date had been changed."

"I bet it was Hamish Bigmore," said Pete. "Probably Wilhelmina Worlock put him up to it."

"That's what I guessed," said Mr Majeika, "and that's what I said to the Silly Crime Squad, but they wouldn't

listen. They said they must take me back to Wizardford-upon-Sky for questioning."

"So up you went on their magic carpet?" asked Thomas.

"Yes," said Mr Majeika. "And when I got there, no one would believe that the date on the licence had been altered, so they said they wouldn't give me a new licence until I had taken my Wizard's Sorcery Exams all over again. They're the tests you have to do before they will give you your licence, just like a driving test."

"Did you mind having to do the exams again?" asked Pete.

"I certainly did," said Mr Majeika. "You see, my magic had got very rusty during the time I'd been teaching at St Barty's. I know you thought I did spells quite often, but most wizards are doing magic full-time, hundreds and hundreds of spells a day, and I was just doing one every few weeks. So really I was forgetting most of what I knew."

"Miss Worlock must have guessed that," said Thomas. "It was all a trick to catch you out, was it?"

"I'm afraid it was," said Mr Majeika. "At first, I was doing all right in the exams. I remembered how to fly, and how to make animals talk, and how to make the moon go backwards across the sky, and all sorts of things like that which are really hard. And then I got caught out by something very simple. The examiner – a tough old wizard called Mugwort – told me to turn myself into a frog. It's a very simple spell, the one I used on Hamish Bigmore when I first came to St Barty's, in fact. But that was the trouble. I remembered what I'd said to make Hamish change, not to make myself change. So maybe you can guess what happened."

"You changed Wizard Mugwort into a frog?" said Pete, laughing.

"That's right," said Mr Majeika. "And I'm afraid Wizard Mugwort didn't see the joke. At least, I don't think he did, because I couldn't manage to turn him back again, and all he could say was 'Gribbet, gribbet!' Look, there he is on the second shelf."

Thomas and Pete looked along the shelf of bottles, until they found one in which a tiny green frog was staring out crossly at them. "But how did you and all the other wizards get made tiny and put into bottles?" asked Thomas.

"I'm coming to that," said Mr Majeika. "Of course I failed the Sorcery Exams on account of making that mistake, and this meant that I had to be punished. It was an awfully long time since anyone else had failed, and the wizards had to look up the correct punishment in a book. They found that people who failed their exams had to be made tiny and put in a bottle for a thousand years."

"A thousand years?" said Thomas. "What a cruel punishment."

"I know," said Mr Majeika, "though a thousand years isn't as long for a wizard as it would be for you – we live to be about ten thousand. Anyway, they didn't remember how to make people small, so small that they could be put into bottles. The only person who said she knew how to do it was –"

"Wilhelmina Worlock?" guessed Pete.

"That's right," said Mr Majeika. "And sure enough she did it, so that I found myself stuck in this bottle. And then – she

did it to all the other wizards! She'd realized that since only she knew how to do that spell, she had them in her power. So of course she didn't hesitate to do it. It meant that she would be the only witch or wizard left full-sized in Wizardford-upon-Sky. She could have the whole place to herself!"

"That's right, dearie," said a familiar voice. Thomas and Pete turned round. Wilhelmina Worlock was standing in the doorway of the Behaviour Changing Factory, grinning all over her horrid face.

6. Wilhelmina Falls in Love

"You nasty little brats," went on Miss
Worlock to Thomas and Pete, "you've got
in my way in the past, and stopped me
triumphing over that weasly little rat,
Majeika, but now nothing and no one can
stop me! Tee hee!"

"I'm afraid she's right," said Mr
Majeika's tiny voice from his bottle. "I'll
simply have to stay here for ever and
ever. Run away, both of you, or she'll do
something nasty to you too."

"Yes, come on, Thomas," said Pete, "let's run." He grabbed Thomas's hand, and dragged him out of the Behaviour Changing Factory and back through the fence to where Mr Majeika's bike was waiting.

"Goodbye and good riddance!" shouted Miss Worlock through the gate. "Don't you ever set foot up here again, or you'll be spending the rest of your lives in bottles, just like the fool Majeika and these stupid wizards."

"We won't," called Pete, getting on to the bike.

"Hey," said Thomas to Pete, "wait a minute. We can't run off and leave Mr Majeika bottled up like that. And we can't leave Jody wandering round here, thinking she's Hamish Bigmore."

"Of course we can't," whispered Pete. "I'm only pretending that we're going."

He shouted out: "Goodbye!" Then he told
Thomas to get on the crossbar of the bike.
"We'll ride it round to the back of
Wizardford," he explained, whispering
again, "because I've got a plan."

When they reached the other side of the
town, Pete and Thomas got off the bike,

and Pete explained his plan. "But why should it be me who has to do all the nasty bits?" complained Thomas. "It ought to be you."

"I thought of it," said Pete firmly, "so I've got to manage it, to organize everything. I need you to do the other things."

Thomas grumbled, but finally he agreed. "So, first we've got to go through this weird fence again, have we?" he asked.

"That's it," said Pete. "In you go." And before Thomas had time to protest again, Pete had pushed him between the bars of the magic fence.

"My whole body is going squidgy again," said Thomas.

"That's the idea," said Pete. "I'm going to change your shape, as if you were a clay model." He began pinching and squeezing bits of Thomas's face, altering the whole appearance of it, and also changing the length of his arms and legs, and the shape of his body.

"So what do I look like now?" asked Thomas, when Pete had finally let him come out of the fence again.

"Haven't you guessed?" said Pete. "You look exactly like – Mr Majeika!" And so he did. Nobody from Class Three would have been able to tell that it wasn't the real Mr Majeika. "Now," went on Pete, "off to the Behaviour Changing Factory. Only we've got to be very careful, in case Wilhelmina Worlock is hanging around there still."

She wasn't. There was no sign of her at all. So Pete and Thomas-who-looked-like-Mr-Majeika hurried inside, and for the next few minutes, Pete kept trying different Behaviour Mixtures on Thomas, until at last he was behaving exactly like Mr Majeika.

"Now," said Pete, "the final stage of the plan. And this is the trickiest."

A few minutes later, Wilhelmina Worlock was strolling up and down in the moonshine at Wizardford, admiring her kingdom, because of course it was all hers now. Suddenly she heard Hamish Bigmore's voice coming from the Love Potion Factory. "Miss Worlock! Miss Worlock! Come and look!"

As it was her Star Pupil calling, Wilhelmina followed the sound of the voice. But when she got into the Love Potion Factory, she discovered that it wasn't Hamish who was calling. It was Jody.

"Well, well, dearie, you sound just like my Star Pupil these days," she said to Jody. "And what are you doing here? You should be on your way back to stupid St Barty's with your little friends."

"I don't want to go back to them," said Jody. "They're silly. I want to stay here, Miss Worlock, and be your servant. I like you so much that I've kept this sweet specially for you!"

Wilhelmina was delighted. It had been hundreds of years since anyone had said they liked her – anyone except Hamish

Bigmore, and he didn't count. "Thank you, dearie," said Wilhelmina, popping the sweet into her mouth. But it wasn't a sweet; it was a lump of sugar.

Jody slipped out of the door. She could still make her voice sound like Hamish's, but she had stopped behaving like him. Pete had brought some Behaviour Mixtures with him, and had managed to get her to drink the right ones to make her sensible again. Once that had been done, she was eager to help with Pete's plan.

Wilhelmina looked around her suspiciously. "Where's that silly little girl vanished to?" she muttered. "And I'm feeling most peculiar."

"Well," said Mr Majeika's voice, "I'm sure I can make you feel better, Wilhelmina. Aren't you glad to see me?" It wasn't the real Mr Majeika; it was Thomas, looking and behaving exactly

like him, who had come through the door
at the back of the Love Potion Factory.

Wilhelmina's eyes lit up. "My love!" she
cooed. "Why did I never notice how
handsome you are! Come to my arms,
you wonderful wizard." *Melisande's
Strongest* had done its work again – Pete
had poured it all over the sugar-lump.

"I will," answered Thomas, "if you will
do one little favour for me."

"Anything in the universe, my heart's desire," spluttered the lovesick Wilhelmina. "Just tell me what, and I shall do it in an instant – and clasp you to my bosom."

Thomas didn't much like the idea of being clasped to Wilhelmina's bosom. He said: "I want you to undo the spell that's put all the wizards in those bottles. Make them all free again, especially Mr Majeika – er, I mean, the one who looks like me."

"Of course, of course, my heaven-sent hero," cooed Wilhelmina, running over to the Behaviour Factory, and taking off the spell at once. About two hundred wizards (one of whom was still in the shape of a frog) climbed out of their bottles and grew back to their normal size.

Of course, the moment they were free again, they grabbed Wilhelmina and took

her to the Wizards' Court, on a charge of
High Treason, Kidnapping, Bottling
People Up, and all sorts of other things.
By this time, Pete had taken Thomas back
to the magic fence, and had squidged him
back to his normal appearance. Thomas
also had a few spoonfuls of Behaviour
Mixture, so that he was entirely returned
to normal.

"I wonder what her punishment will be," he said to Mr Majeika.

"They're letting me decide," said Mr Majeika, "as they've realized that she cheated me over the Wizard's Licence. I'm trying to think of the most suitable punishment for her. Ah – I know."

"What will you choose, Mr Majeika?" asked Jody, following him into the courtroom. "Banish her to outer darkness? Lock her up in the deepest dungeon in the world?"

"You'll hear in a moment, Jody," said Mr Majeika. "Now, Wilhelmina," he said to Miss Worlock, who was being guarded by two very ferocious witches, "I have decided that your punishment will be to do a spell –"

"A spell? Oh, I'll do any kind of spell you want," said Miss Worlock hopefully.

"Let me finish," said Mr Majeika

sternly. "Your punishment will be to do a
'spell' on Earth – that's to say, a length of
time – as a Supply Teacher. And without
being able to do any magic!"

"A Supply Teacher?" spluttered
Wilhelmina. "What's that?"

"It's someone who comes to take a class
when the regular teacher is away," said
Thomas.

"Oh no!" gasped Wilhelmina. "Teaching

lots of children I don't know – that would be quite exhausting."

"And no magic," said Mr Majeika firmly. "Absolutely no magic."

There was a roar of laughter from the back of the courtroom. Hamish Bigmore, far from caring that Miss Worlock was in trouble, thought that Mr Majeika's punishment was very funny.

So next time your regular teacher is away, and someone strange comes to teach you, watch out! It could be Wilhelmina Worlock.

Also in Young Puffin

Mr Majeika

and the

Haunted Hotel

Humphrey Carpenter

Spooks and spectres at the *Green Banana*!

Class Three of St Barty's are off on an outing to Hadrian's Wall with their teacher, Mr Majeika (who happens to be a magician). Stranded in the fog when the tyres of their coach are mysteriously punctured, they take refuge in a nearby hotel called the Green Banana. Soon some very spooky things start to happen. Strange lights, ghostly sounds and vanishing people...

Also in Young Puffin

Mr Majeika

and the

MUSIC TEACHER

Humphrey Carpenter

**"Music teacher? What music teacher?
I don't know anything about any
music teacher."**

It's a new term at St Barty's and the
school is in uproar. Awful noises come
from Class Three, angry parents fill the
school and poor Mr Majeika is really
frightened. Why? A new music teacher
is coming who plans to start a school
orchestra, and as only Mr Majeika
knows, Wilhelmina Worlock is
a witch!

Also in Young Puffin

MR MAJEIKA
and the
SCHOOL INSPECTOR

Humphrey Carpenter

"Use of magic by teacher strictly forbidden."

Poor Mr Majeika gains so many penalty points when the nasty Mr Postlethwaite, a school inspector, comes to inspect St Barty's School that he very nearly loses his teacher's licence. However, at Barty Castle Mr Majeika gets his revenge when he arranges for the inspector to have a very chilling encounter.

Yet more hilarities occur when Mr Majeika accidently turns himself into a lobster and Class Three have to trick Wilhelmina Worlock into undoing the spell. And troublesome Hamish Bigmore gets a fright when another version of the class nuisance magically appears to put him in order!

MR MAJEIKA
and the
SCHOOL BOOK WEEK

Humphrey Carpenter

"Gosh," said Thomas, "isn't that Robin Hood?"

When St Barty's School have their Book Week, you can be sure that Mr Majeika brings the characters alive – but how can he make them go back into their books? And when a new PE teacher organizes an Olympic Sports Day and has Hamish Bigmore winning every event – there has to be magic in the air.

In the third story, Class Three go to France and Hamish is a real pain! Mr Majeika just wishes he could cast spells in French . . . or does he?

More adventures starring everyone's favourite wizard.

MR MAJEIKA'S
POSTBAG

Humphrey Carpenter

**Majeika calling! Majeika calling!
Help needed!**

Follow the antics of your favourite
wizard as he helps save a family of foxes,
narrowly escapes having to marry an
ugly mermaid and lends Santa a hand in
the festive season.

As well as stories, there are jokes,
Walpurgian recipes and secret coded
messages in Mr Majeika's postbag – a
wizard of a book!

READ MORE IN PUFFIN

For children of all ages, Puffin represents quality and variety – the very best in publishing today around the world.

For complete information about books available from Puffin – and Penguin – and how to order them, contact us at the appropriate address below. Please note that for copyright reasons the selection of books varies from country to country.

On the worldwide web: www.puffin.co.uk

In the United Kingdom: Please write to *Dept. EP, Penguin Books Ltd, Bath Road, Harmondsworth, West Drayton, Middlesex UB7 ODA*

In the United States: Please write to *Consumer Sales, Penguin USA, P.O. Box 999, Dept. 17109, Bergenfield, New Jersey 07621-0120.* VISA and MasterCard holders call 1-800-253-6476 to order Penguin titles

In Canada: Please write to *Penguin Books Canada Ltd, 10 Alcorn Avenue, Suite 300, Toronto, Ontario M4V 3B2*

In Australia: Please write to *Penguin Books Australia Ltd, P.O. Box 257, Ringwood, Victoria 3134*

In New Zealand: Please write to *Penguin Books (NZ) Ltd, Private Bag 102902, North Shore Mail Centre, Auckland 10*

In India: Please write to *Penguin Books India Pvt Ltd, 706 Eros Apartments, 56 Nehru Place, New Delhi 110 019*

In the Netherlands: Please write to *Penguin Books Netherlands bv, Postbus 3507, NL-1001 AH Amsterdam*

In Germany: Please write to *Penguin Books Deutschland GmbH, Metzlerstrasse 26, 60594 Frankfurt am Main*

In Spain: Please write to *Penguin Books S. A., Bravo Murillo 19, 1° B, 28015 Madrid*

In Italy: Please write to *Penguin Italia s.r.l., Via Felice Casati 20, I -20124 Milano.*

In France: Please write to *Penguin France S. A., 17 rue Lejeune, F-31000 Toulouse*

In Japan: Please write to *Penguin Books Japan, Ishikiribashi Building, 2–5–4, Suido, Bunkyo-ku, Tokyo 112*

In South Africa: Please write to *Longman Penguin Southern Africa (Pty) Ltd, Private Bag X08, Bertsham 2013*